For David and Amelia
M.W.

For Charlie
B.F.

Text copyright © 1991 by Martin Waddell
Illustrations copyright © 1991 by Barbara Firth

First U.S. paperback edition 1995

Library of Congress Cataloging-in-Publication Data

Waddell, Martin.
Let's go home, Little Bear / by Martin Waddell ; illustrated by
Barbara Firth.—1st U.S. ed.
Summary: When Little Bear is frightened by the noises he hears while
walking in the snowy woods, his friend Big Bear reassures him.
ISBN 1-56402-131-9 (harcover)—ISBN 1-56402-447-4 (paperback)
[1. Bears—Fiction. 2. Fear—Fiction. 3. Noise—Fiction.]
I. Firth, Barbara, ill. II. Title.
PZ7.W1137Ld   1993   92-53003
[E]—dc20

2 4 6 8 10 9 7 5 3

Printed in Hong Kong

The pictures in this book were
done in watercolor.

Candlewick Press
2067 Massachusetts Avenue
Cambridge, Massachusetts 02140

LET'S GO HOME, LITTLE BEAR

by
Martin Waddell

illustrated by
Barbara Firth

CANDLEWICK PRESS
CAMBRIDGE, MASSACHUSETTS

Once there were two bears.

Big Bear and Little Bear.

Big Bear is the big bear

and Little Bear is the little bear.

They went for a walk in the woods.

They walked and they walked and
they walked until Big Bear said,
"Let's go home, Little Bear."
So they started back home on the
path through the woods.

PLOD PLOD PLOD

went Big Bear, plodding along.

Little Bear ran on in front,

jumping and sliding

and having great fun.

And then . . .

Little Bear stopped

and he listened

and then he turned around

and he looked.

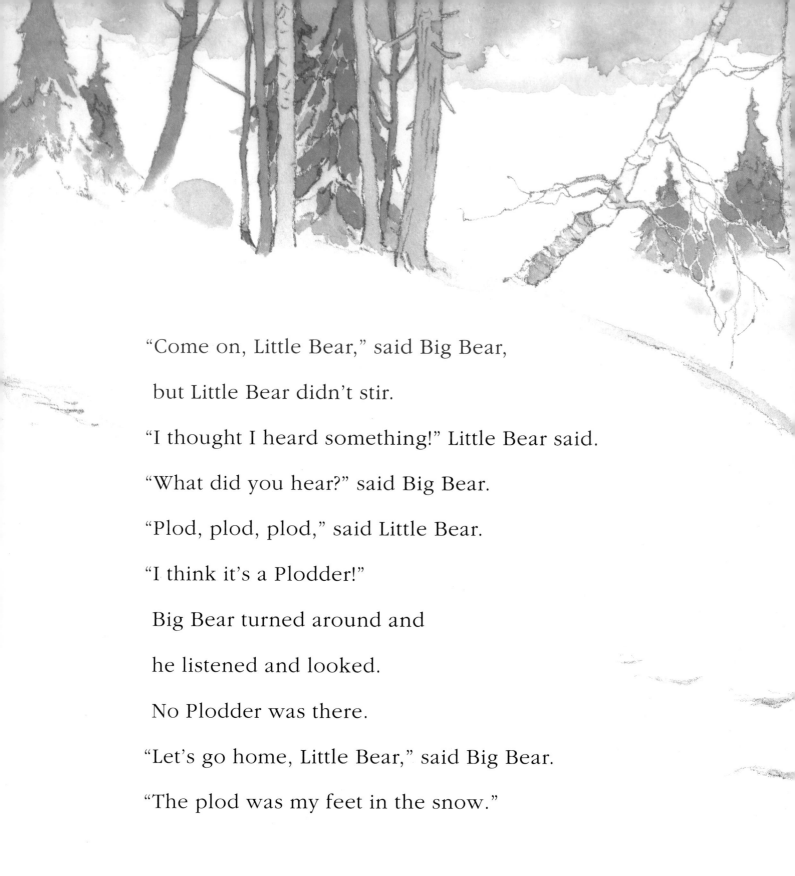

"Come on, Little Bear," said Big Bear,

but Little Bear didn't stir.

"I thought I heard something!" Little Bear said.

"What did you hear?" said Big Bear.

"Plod, plod, plod," said Little Bear.

"I think it's a Plodder!"

Big Bear turned around and

he listened and looked.

No Plodder was there.

"Let's go home, Little Bear," said Big Bear.

"The plod was my feet in the snow."

They set off again on the path

through the woods.

P L O D   P L O D   P L O D

went Big Bear with Little Bear

walking beside him,

just glancing a bit, now and again.

And then . . .

Little Bear stopped

and he listened

and then he turned around

and he looked.

"Come on, Little Bear," said Big Bear,

but Little Bear didn't stir.

"I thought I heard something!"

Little Bear said.

"What did you hear?" said Big Bear.

"Drip, drip, drip," said Little Bear.

"I think it's a Dripper!"

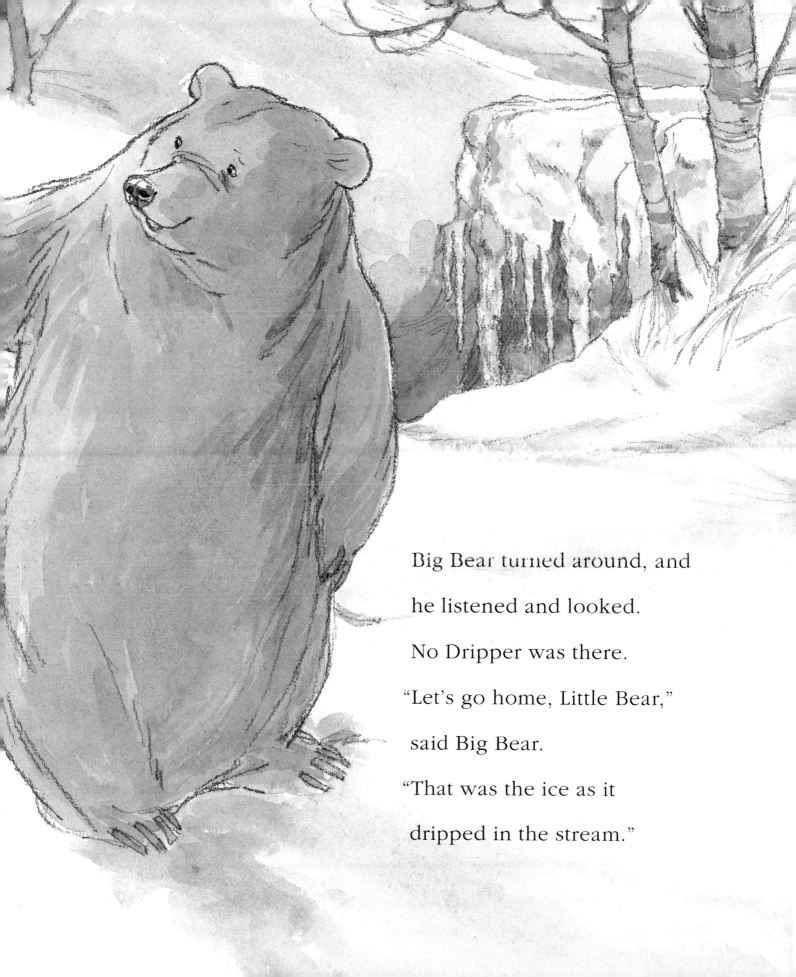

Big Bear turned around, and
he listened and looked.
No Dripper was there.
"Let's go home, Little Bear,"
said Big Bear.
"That was the ice as it
dripped in the stream."

They set off again on the

path through the woods.

PLOD PLOD PLOD

went Big Bear with Little Bear

closer beside him.

And then . . .

Little Bear stopped

and he listened

and then he turned around

and he looked.

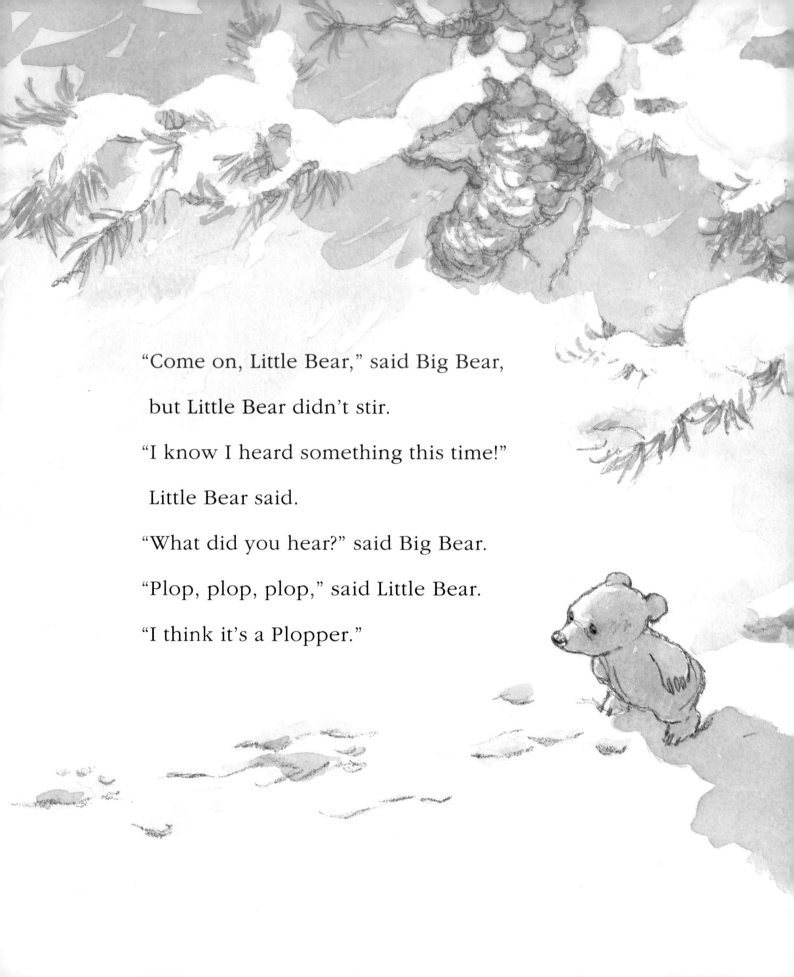

"Come on, Little Bear," said Big Bear,

but Little Bear didn't stir.

"I know I heard something this time!"

Little Bear said.

"What did you hear?" said Big Bear.

"Plop, plop, plop," said Little Bear.

"I think it's a Plopper."

Big Bear turned around,

and he listened and looked.

No Plopper was there.

"Let's go home, Little Bear,"

said Big Bear.

"That was the snow plopping

down from a branch."

PLOD PLOD PLOD

went Big Bear along the path

through the woods.

But Little Bear walked

slower and slower

and at last he sat

down in the snow.

"Come on, Little Bear," said Big Bear.

"It is time we were both back home."

But Little Bear sat and said nothing.

"Come on and be carried,"

said Big Bear.

Big Bear put Little Bear

high up on his back

and set off down the path

through the woods.

WOO WOO WOO

"It is only the wind, Little Bear,"

said Big Bear and he walked

on down the path.

CREAK CREAK CREAK

"It is only the trees, Little Bear,"

said Big Bear and he walked

on down the path.

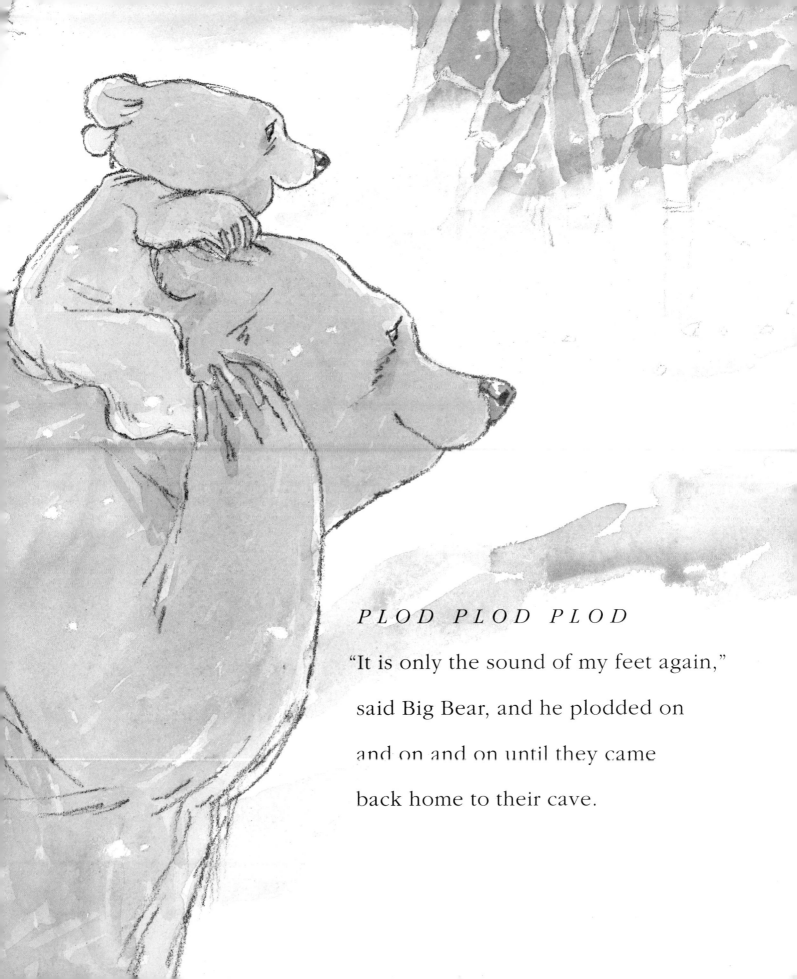

PLOD PLOD PLOD

"It is only the sound of my feet again,"

said Big Bear, and he plodded on

and on and on until they came

back home to their cave.

Big Bear and Little Bear

went down into the dark,

the dark of their own

Bear Cave.

"Just stay there, Little Bear,"

said Big Bear, putting Little Bear

in the Bear Chair with a blanket

to keep him warm.

Big Bear stirred up the fire

from the embers

and lighted the lamps

and made the Bear Cave

all cozy again.

"Now tell me a story,"

Little Bear said.

And Big Bear sat down in the Bear Chair

with Little Bear curled up on his lap.

And he told a story of Plodders

and Drippers and Ploppers

and the sounds of the snow

in the woods,

and this Little Bear

and this Big Bear

plodding all the way . . .

HOME